MW00905231

The Let's Talk Library™

Let's Talk About
Having Chicken Pox

Elizabeth Weitzman

The Rosen Publishing Group's
PowerKids Press™
New York

Published in 1997 by The Rosen Publishing Group, Inc.
29 East 21st Street, New York, NY 10010

First Edition

Book Design: Erin McKenna

Photo Illustrations: front cover © 1993 Martin/Custom Medical Stock; pp. 4, 8, 11, 12, 15, 19, 20 by Seth Dinnerman; p. 7 © 1996 Martin/Custom Medical Stock; p. 16 by Sarah Friedman.

Weitzman, Elizabeth.
    Let's talk about having chicken pox / Elizabeth Weitzman.
        p.   cm. — (The Let's talk library)
    Includes index.
    Summary: Explains what causes the chicken pox, how you feel when you have it, and what can be done to treat this disease.
    ISBN 0-8239-5031-X (lib. bdg.)
    1. Chicken pox—Juvenile literature. [1. Chicken pox. 2. Diseases.] I. Title. II. Series.
RC125.W45 1996
616.9'14—dc20
                                                         96-43326
                                                           CIP
                                                           AC

Manufactured in the United States of America

Contents

Sam

One morning Sam woke up and stared at his arm in surprise. It was covered with itchy, red spots. What was the matter with him? He ran down the stairs to show his dad.

"Uh-oh," his father said as he took the **thermometer** (ther-MOM-ih-ter) out of Sam's mouth. "You have a **fever** (FEE-ver)." He checked the spots on Sam's arm again. "You'd better get back in bed. You've got chicken pox."

◄ Chicken pox may first show up on your arm, chest, or back.

5

What Is Chicken Pox?

Usually, your body is able to fight off harmful **germs** (JERMZ). A germ is a living thing so small that you can't even see millions of them put together. Many illnesses are caused by germs called **viruses** (VY-rus-ez). Chicken pox is one of those illnesses. Viruses move from one person to another very quickly. When one kid gets a virus, lots of others do too. Nearly every child gets chicken pox. Luckily, most people have it only once.

Chicken pox is caused by a virus. ▶
Many people get chicken pox.

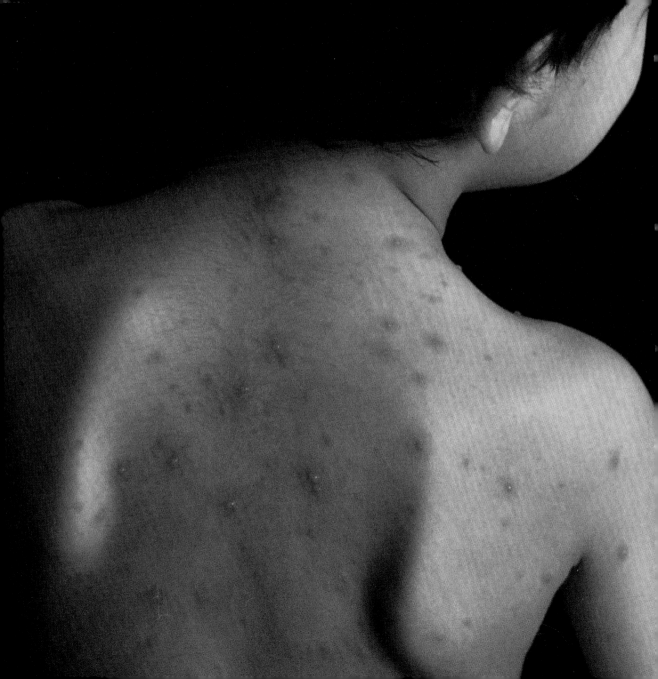

It's Easy to Catch

The reason so many kids get chicken pox is that it's very easy to catch from someone else. Chicken pox germs usually enter your body through your nose and mouth. They might be in the air, or on toys or other things used by a sick person. To help stop germs from making you sick, always wash your hands before you eat. Also, be sure to cover your mouth whenever you sneeze or cough. This will keep your germs from getting on others.

◀ Protect yourself and others by covering your mouth when you sneeze or cough.

When You Have Chicken Pox

When you first have chicken pox, you'll notice red spots on your body. Then you may start to feel pretty bad. You might have a headache and a fever, and feel very tired. After a few days, the red spots will turn into itchy **blisters** (BLIS-terz). Then the blisters become scabs. Just like the scabs you get when you scrape your knee, these will fall off after a few days.

It's important to rest when ▶
you have chicken pox.

Scratching

Chicken pox blisters are usually very itchy. You'll want to scratch them, but don't do it! First of all, if you pick at a blister or scab, it can leave a lasting **scar** (SKAR). The blisters and scabs will go away in a couple of weeks, but a scar can last for months or even the rest of your life. Second, although it seems like scratching will make you feel better, that's not really true. It will actually make the blisters worse, which can hurt you.

◀ Scratching chicken pox blisters will make them worse, and could even cause more blisters to form.

How Can You Feel Better?

There are things you can do to feel better. Be sure to get plenty of rest. You don't have to lie in bed the whole time. However, you do need to take it easy and stay at home.

To help the itching, try taking a lot of baths. Make sure the water is lukewarm—neither hot nor cold, but right in the middle. Your parents may also rub some lotion on your blisters. This will help them heal faster.

Putting lotion on your blisters
can stop them from itching. ▶

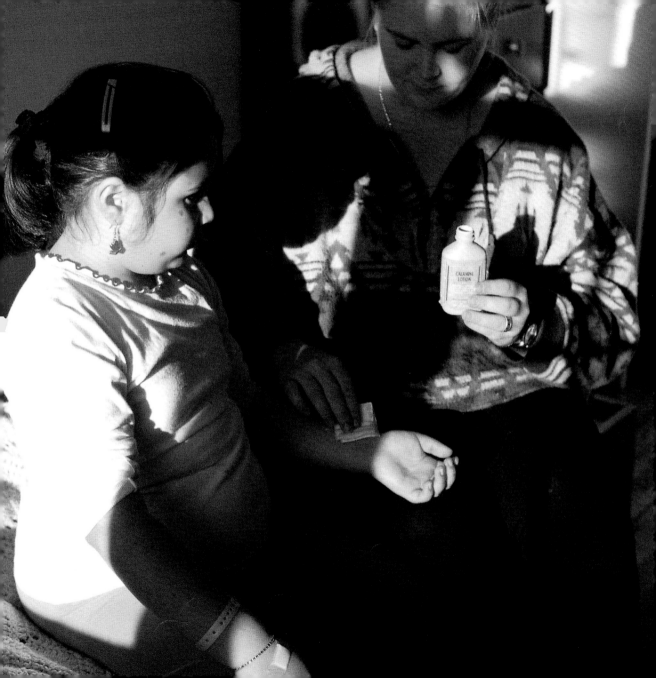

Medicine

Your parents may give you some medicine to make you feel better. This will help if you have a fever or a headache. It may also help the itching. It's important to take the medicine your parents give you. But don't take any medicine by yourself. You should take medicine only when your parents give it to you.

◀ If you have a bad headache or a fever, your parents may give you some medicine to make you feel better.

Staying at Home

You'll have to stay at home for a couple of weeks while you have chicken pox. There's no reason for you to be bored, though. Your friends might be able to drop off your schoolwork every day. Find out if someone can take books out of the library for you. Ask your mom or dad to get you some paper, crayons, and pens. Then you can even write your own book about anything you want. You might even write about what it's like to have chicken pox.

There are lots of different things you can do ▶
while you are getting over chicken pox.

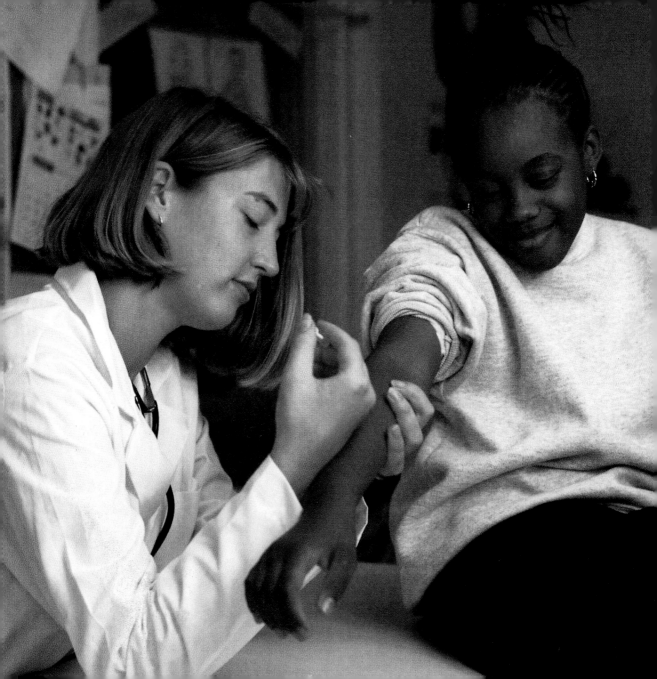

The Chicken Pox Vaccine

Pretty soon most kids won't get chicken pox anymore. That's because doctors are giving their **patients** (PAY-shents) a chicken pox **vaccine** (vax-EEN). A vaccine is usually given as a shot. The shot stings for a minute, but then it stops hurting. The vaccine helps your body learn how to fight the chicken pox virus.

◀ A chicken pox vaccine will protect your body against the virus.

It Will Be Over Soon

When you first get chicken pox, you might feel bad and itchy all over. However, the blisters will itch less and less as the days go by. You'll still have some scabs after they stop itching, but after a while you won't even notice them. Then one day you'll wake up and they'll all be gone. And chances are, you won't ever have to worry about having chicken pox again!

Glossary

blister (BLIS-ter) A small bubble on your skin filled with liquid.

fever (FEE-ver) A rise in your body heat.

germ (JERM) Tiny living thing that can cause sickness.

patient (PAY-shent) A person who goes to the doctor.

scar (SKAR) A mark left by a cut, burn, or sore.

thermometer (ther-MOM-ih-ter) Tool used to measure how hot or how cold a person's body is.

vaccine (vax-EEN) A protection against a sickness, usually given as a shot.

virus (VY-rus) A type of germ.

Index